A Time to Be Brave

"Well, well, what do we have here?" asked one of the soldiers. He blocked my way. He was tall, with a thin, mean mouth. His friend had eyes like ice.

"Open up. Let's see what you have."

With trembling fingers, I unfastened the box.

A Time to Be Brave

previously published as *Honey Cake*

by **Joan Betty Stuchner**

illustrated by **Cynthia Nugent**

A STEPPING STONE BOOK™

Random House 🏠 New York

Text copyright © 2007 by Joan Betty Stuchner
Interior illustrations copyright © 2007 by Cynthia Nugent
Cover art copyright © 2014 by Chris Beatrice

All photos in "The Story Behind the Story" courtesy of the Museum of Danish Resistance.

All rights reserved. This 2014 edition was published in the United States by Random House Children's Books, a division of Random House LLC, a Penguin Random House Company, New York. Originally published in hardcover as *Honey Cake* in Canada and Great Britain by Tradewind Books, Vancouver, BC, in 2007 and in the United States by Random House Children's Books, New York, in 2008.

Random House and the colophon are registered trademarks and A Stepping Stone Book and the colophon are trademarks of Random House LLC.

Visit us on the Web!
SteppingStonesBooks.com
randomhouse.com/kids

Educators and librarians, for a variety of teaching tools,
visit us at RHTeachersLibrarians.com

Library of Congress Cataloging-in-Publication Data is available upon request.
ISBN 978-0-385-39205-1 (pbk.) — ISBN 978-0-385-39206-8 (ebook)

Printed in the United States of America
10 9 8 7 6 5 4 3 2 1

This book has been officially leveled by using the F&P Text Level Gradient™ Leveling System.

*This book is for Tom Kavadias and Dov Stuchner-Kavadias.
It is also for the people of Denmark and Sweden, and in
memory of His Majesty King Christian X of Denmark.
—J.B.S.*

*For Margret Schäfer and Marie Aubin, who took care
of me in Berlin, put me on the bus to Copenhagen,
and made history come alive for me.
—C.N.*

ACKNOWLEDGMENTS

Thanks to Bente Nathan Thomsen—her story inspired this book. Thanks also to Cindy Heinrichs, Cynthia Nugent, Michael Katz, and Carol Frank. Thanks again to Rick Welch.

CONTENTS

One

Copenhagen, September 6, 1943

"David," Mama called. "Time to get up."

I thought I was dreaming, but when I opened my eyes I realized that it really was a school day. A ray of sunlight poked out from beneath the heavy blackout drapes. Before the occupation my window drapes had been pale blue and much nicer. Breakfast smells reached me, and I jumped out of bed and opened the drapes.

It was early autumn, and the leaves on

some of the trees had begun to turn from green to yellow. Soon they'd be orange, then red. I had hoped that by the time Jewish New Year came around, the leaves would form a crunchy brown carpet covering the streets of Copenhagen. Autumn is my favorite time of year. Of course, Copenhagen is the most beautiful city in the world, any time of year. Even Nazi soldiers couldn't make Copenhagen ugly.

That morning, over breakfast, Mama said, "I'll bake a honey cake for Rosh Hashanah to make the New Year sweet." My big sister, Rachel, and I bit into our slices of dry toast. Breakfasts weren't as tasty since the Nazis had occupied Denmark. They sent most of our good food to Germany. Still, as Papa told us whenever we complained, "In other occupied countries people suffer much more than we do here in Denmark."

Rachel washed down the toast with chicory coffee and pulled a face. Rationing had put an end to real coffee. "A sweet year," she said, "would be a year without Nazis."

Mama nodded. "It would also be wonderful to have real coffee again," she said.

Rachel and I laughed as Mama poured her cup of chicory coffee into the sink.

"Why doesn't Papa bake the honey cake?" I asked with a straight face. I didn't mean to suggest that Papa could make better cakes. But after all, he *was* a baker.

Mama gave me a sharp look. "I'll have you know, David, that your papa's not the only member of the Nathan family who can bake cakes."

Rachel winked at me across the table. Nathan's Patisserie, Papa's pastry shop downstairs, was still the best in Copenhagen, even though good ingredients were getting harder and harder to find. His assistant, Mrs. Jensen, had a seaside cottage in Humlebaek. Some of her neighbors there ran small farms. They secretly sold Papa butter and fresh cream. If the soldiers found out, they would be very angry.

Most of the time Mama took care of the

apartment. On weekday afternoons, if it got busy in the pastry shop, she helped serve behind the counter. Still, even though Mama didn't bake for the shop, no one in the world made a tastier honey cake. She only baked it once a year for Rosh Hashanah. Papa was the first to admit, "When it comes to honey cake, children, your mama beats me hands down." So I suppose that's why we'd never tasted Papa's.

As I ate the last bit of dry toast, I pretended it was Mama's honey cake. My mouth watered.

Rachel checked her watch and got up quickly. "I have to go," she said, picking up her schoolbooks and coat.

"So early?" said Mama with a frown.

Rachel was always in a hurry these days. She left home early and came home late. Sometimes she didn't come home at all.

"I have to give Papa something," she said.

Mama looked worried as Rachel kissed her goodbye. "Bye, David," Rachel said to me. But she looked as if her thoughts were already miles away.

After Rachel had gone, Mama said very little. There was no point in my asking questions. Whenever I mentioned that Rachel was hardly ever home, Mama would say, "She has to study hard at the university, David. There's a lot of pressure, with papers to write and final exams to worry about."

The old Rachel wouldn't have been so serious, even about exams. On the other hand, it seemed as if the whole world had become serious, waiting for the worst to happen. Only what could be worse than being occupied? What could be worse than not being free?

I finished my breakfast and helped Mama wash the dishes.

"Will the Jensens eat Rosh Hashanah dinner with us as usual?" I asked.

"Of course," said Mama. "The Jensens are family." Mama always said that everyone in Denmark was like family. That didn't stop us from missing our real family. They'd moved to England before the war.

Aunt Bente, Uncle Leo, Cousin Lars, and even Grandma lived in London. Sometimes they sent letters. They planned to return to Copenhagen when the war was over. I knew they must be very homesick.

"Elsa's probably waiting for you in the pastry shop," said Mama. I kissed her and ran downstairs.

Elsa was Mrs. Jensen's daughter. She was also my classmate and best friend. Her father owned the toy shop next door. Elsa thought that I was lucky my father owned a pastry shop. But I thought she was the lucky one.

Every morning I looked in the window of Jensen's Toys to see if the train set was still there. My tenth birthday was coming in November, and all I wanted was that train. But what if Mr. Jensen sold it before then? Anything could happen in two months.

Halfway down the back stairs I could smell the warm fragrance of freshly baked cookies. I quickened my step. Papa and Mrs. Jensen had been baking since before sunrise.

"There he is," said Mrs. Jensen as I opened the back door. She patted her big white apron, setting free a small floury cloud. "You're just in time." Then she handed me a sugar-speckled cookie from a tray on the counter like she did every day before school. It was still warm from the oven. Elsa grinned at me as she licked crumbs from her fingertips.

"Thank you, Mrs. Jensen," I said. The cookie was sweet, much tastier than dry toast.

"Good morning, David," said Papa. He stepped out from the baking area, carrying a tray of cream-filled chocolate éclairs. Elsa and I stared in amazement. It had been a long time since Papa had made éclairs.

As Papa put the six éclairs in a box, he noticed our surprise. He exchanged glances with Mrs. Jensen, as if they shared a secret.

"These are a special order," he murmured. That was another thing that the occupation had brought—grown-ups always seemed to have secrets.

Papa checked his pocket watch. "Someone should be picking them up soon." He looked worried, the way Mama had when Rachel left that morning. Whatever could be so serious about chocolate éclairs?

As I opened the front door, the bells above

it jingled. Elsa and I said goodbye to Papa and Mrs. Jensen and left the shop's warm, comforting smells.

As usual there were two Nazi soldiers standing on the corner. These two sometimes came into the shop and took pastries without paying. Some soldiers at least paid for what they took. Still, no one liked any of them, even the polite ones. Denmark was *our* country, not theirs.

It had been three years since the Nazis had invaded. At first Elsa and I were scared of the soldiers, but we soon got used to them. We didn't like them, but we grew accustomed to the sight of armed men in uniforms patrolling the streets, parks, and railway station. I knew we wouldn't have to put up with them forever. I'd heard my parents and the Jensens talking. They said that someday, when the

Allies won the war, the Nazis would leave Denmark. Then we'd be free again. No more blackouts. No more air raids. No more chicory coffee.

"After all," reasoned Elsa, "it's lots of countries against just one. I'm surprised they've taken so long, aren't you?"

I said yes, but I was sure there must be some reason why we'd waited three years. Elsa and I had been warned not to ever talk about the Allies or mention the war. Papa said that soldiers were trained to listen to gossip.

I asked him, "Is it all right if we think about it?" Papa smiled and said everyone was free to think, and Elsa and I should go ahead and think whatever we wanted.

"But always remember," Papa warned, "walls have ears. And sometimes trees do too." And he grinned and ruffled my hair with his floury hand.

For a long time I had dreams about that. Walls and trees with large, flapping ears. But that was when I was little. Now it was 1943, and I was almost ten.

Elsa and I waited patiently for the Allies to save Denmark. We didn't talk about it, because of the walls and trees having ears. But I knew we were both thinking the same thing. One day we'd look outside, and instead of the Nazi flag, we'd see the Danish flag, the beautiful Dannebrog. One day.

Two

Copenhagen, May 5, 1940

When we were very young, Elsa and I sometimes forgot that the soldiers were dangerous enemies. Once, almost a month after the occupation began, we were playing in the street when two soldiers walked by. They almost stepped on the toy cars we were racing. One soldier's big black boot kicked my car into the gutter. He didn't even say sorry. We watched angrily as the two men continued down the street.

Suddenly I had an idea. Grinning at Elsa, I stood up and followed, at a safe distance, copying the soldiers' stiff movements. Elsa soon joined in the fun. The two of us goose-stepped down the street behind the soldiers, who didn't suspect a thing. We pretended we had rifles over our shoulders and even gave the silly salute we'd often seen other soldiers give to each other. It was difficult not to think them funny. We didn't imagine what might happen if the soldiers saw us.

Our joke
ended quite abruptly.

We didn't see Mr. Jen-
sen come out of his shop.
We didn't hear his quick step
behind us. Before we knew it, we were being
propelled into the doorway of Jensen's Toys.
He turned us around to face him. I'd never
seen such an angry expression on his usually
kind face.

"David, Elsa, war is not a game. Do you
understand me?"

We nodded.

"Yes, Mr. Jensen."

"Yes, Papa."

"And will you do anything so foolish again?"

"No, Mr. Jensen."

"No, Papa."

"Next time I'll have to tell your parents, David. Do you understand me?"

I nodded. It wasn't just that I was afraid of getting into trouble. I'd noticed how upset my parents had been since the Nazi invasion of Denmark. I didn't want to make things worse.

Three

Copenhagen, April 9, 1940: The Invasion

I will never forget the day the Nazis invaded. Grown-ups say that children forget things from when they're little. That's not true. Some things you can't forget. It was three years ago, just before Passover.

Passover is usually the time when Jews celebrate being freed from slavery. This Passover no Danes would be free—Christians *or* Jews.

Mama had been cleaning the apartment to get ready for Passover. The Jensens would celebrate with us at our seder. Our families usually shared holidays. At Christmas the Jensens let me help trim their tree, and at Easter they always gave me a big sugared egg. In turn, my parents always invited the Jensens over for Jewish holidays. As Mama says, everyone in Denmark is family.

Mama had hung the living room carpet on the clothesline in the courtyard. She was smacking it with the carpet beater that always reminded me of a tennis racket. Every time Mama hit the carpet, a cloud of dust flew up into the clear blue sky. The air smelled of flowers, budding beech trees, and carpet dust. On such a day it was hard to imagine the rest of Europe was at war. Elsa and I were sitting on the step watching Mama. Now and then we sneezed from the dust. The only other sound was a distant *shush* of traffic on the main road.

Then we heard it. Like a drone of giant bees in the distance. Mama stopped beating and wiped one arm across her forehead. The ground began to vibrate. I ran to her. Mrs. Jensen rushed outside and grabbed Elsa's hand. Even Papa left the shop to see what was happening.

Was it the end of the world?

The droning grew louder. Now it sounded like the growl of a vicious dog. I pushed my fingers into my ears as neighbors ran out into the street. Everyone looked up at the sky. Then we saw them. Hundreds of airplanes, like giant vultures, flying low, blocking out the sun. I noticed a strange marking on each plane. It looked like a twisted cross.

"What's that shape?" I shouted above the roar.

"The swastika," said Mama. She held me tighter.

"What does it mean?"

"It means," Mama said, "that the Nazis have invaded Denmark. God help us all."

I'd heard stories about the Nazis. I knew they hated Jews. Their leader was Adolf Hitler. Mama said that Hitler wanted to rule the whole world.

Later that day I overheard Mama whisper to Papa, "What are we going to do?"

"Let's wait and see," answered Papa.

"Let's not wait too long," said Mama.

At first the Danes, even Jewish Danes, were not mistreated as much as people in other occupied countries were. Every day King Christian proudly rode his horse through Copenhagen. Papa said it was to reassure his people and to defy the Nazis. It helped us to be brave. But nothing was quite the same. And now, three years later, the Nazis were still in Denmark.

Four

Copenhagen, September 6, 1943

As we left for school that morning, I wondered if we had time to walk to Tivoli Gardens to see the king. But first I glanced into the window of Jensen's Toys. The train set—*my* train set—was in the window. It chugged around the track, with smoke puffing from the engine's chimney, and its headlight beamed. I prayed it wouldn't be sold before my birthday.

"Do you think we have time to see the king?" I asked Elsa.

"If we hurry," she said, grabbing my hand and pulling me. We ran as fast as we could, crossing the road to avoid the soldiers.

The king was early that day, and the crowd was larger than usual. As he rode along Vesterbrogade, the king nodded to his right and left. He even stopped to shake hands with an elderly man. The man wore a shabby overcoat, but pinned to the top pocket were some medals.

"He must have been a soldier once," whispered Elsa.

After shaking hands, the old soldier and the king saluted each other.

There were about fifty people standing on our side of the street. Now it was my turn to pull Elsa. "Quick," I said, "let's get closer."

We made our way through the crowd until we were a few yards away from the king and his horse. Suddenly there was silence. Four German soldiers had appeared out of nowhere. They marched down the street, stood to attention before the king, and gave the Nazi salute. Everyone gasped, and anger was written on every face—except the king's. His face didn't betray any emotion. I held my breath and tightened my grip on Elsa's hand.

The king looked at the soldiers for a moment, turned his horse, and rode off in the opposite direction.

As Elsa and I ran to school, the cheers of approval still rang in our ears. We couldn't wait to tell our teacher, Miss Kiersted.

Miss Kiersted let us tell the class about seeing the king that morning. She nodded. "The king is a brave and honorable man. He loves his people." We all wanted to talk more about the king and the occupation, but Miss Kiersted clapped her hands for quiet. "Despite the occupation and all the bad things happening in the world, we still have to carry on. When all of you grow up, you will make the world a much better place."

Then we rehearsed our class play. Miss Kiersted had written it. It was based on the story "The Little Mermaid" by our great Danish writer Hans Christian Andersen. I want to be a writer just like him. One of my stories was selected for the school magazine. It was about a boy who can paint pictures that come alive. It wasn't about me. I'm not a very good artist. When Papa read my story, he laughed and said, "Stories are magic, David. With your writing you can make anything happen."

I couldn't wait until the end of October, when the magazine came out. Everyone in the school would get a copy, and I could finally see my story in print.

Elsa was more excited than I was about the class play. That's because she wants to be an actress someday. She *is* very good. Naturally, Miss Kiersted picked her to be the mermaid. Still, despite the fun of being part of a play—I was one of the sardines—something bothered me. Something I needed to talk about with Papa.

After school Elsa and I walked past Tivoli Gardens again. Elsa liked the flowers, but I loved the carousel that spun like a giant music box.

"Mama's making honey cake. She says it's for a sweet new year," I said.

"A sweet year," said Elsa, "would be a year without the Nazis."

I looked at her, surprised. "That's exactly what Rachel said." Elsa gave me a strange smile. We reached our street and crossed at the corner. When we saw the two soldiers at the other end, Elsa pulled me aside.

"David, I have a secret. Promise not to tell!"

I promised.

"Rachel and my cousin Arne are in the Resistance. They blow up buildings and railroad tracks. I heard my parents talking one night."

I stared at her. "But Rachel's a girl!"

Elsa frowned at me. "Girls can fight too," she said. "If the Nazis are still here when I'm older, I'll join the Resistance too."

No wonder my parents always looked worried. Rachel was in danger. And it explained why she hardly ever spent time at home anymore. It had nothing to do with university exams at all.

I knew about the Resistance. They printed illegal newspapers denouncing the Nazis. They committed acts of sabotage against the soldiers, blowing up buildings used by the enemy. Other Danes, like Miss Kiersted, defied the Germans by wearing caps knitted in the colors of our flag—the white and red Dannebrog. Still others held *alsangs* in parks and squares. They sang patriotic songs and Danish folk songs to boost our morale.

When the Germans figured out what was

happening, they banned all public *alsangs*.

I also knew that some of my older school-mates were involved in causing trouble for the Nazis. A few of them ran errands for the underground. Others put sugar into the gas tanks of army trucks. I admired their courage. But it didn't make the soldiers go away.

Papa looked startled as the bell over the door jingled. When he saw Elsa and me, he looked relieved. "David, I have an errand for you."

Mrs. Jensen rushed forward. "Elsa, your father needs us right away to help with something." Elsa began to protest, but Mrs. Jensen ushered her out of the pastry shop.

When they were gone, Papa handed me a box. "No one came for the éclairs, David. I need you to deliver them to Elsa's cousin Arne." He made me memorize the address.

"David, this is a very special delivery. It's

important that they *all* get there safely." He looked at me seriously. At first I was confused. Then I understood. My mouth felt dry. My heart was pounding.

"I'll do it."

Carefully holding the box in my arms, I walked toward the end of the block. The two soldiers were still on the corner. I didn't even look at my train.

"Well, well, what do we have here?" asked one of the soldiers. He blocked my way. He was tall, with a thin, mean mouth. His friend had eyes like ice.

"Open up. Let's see what you have."

With trembling fingers, I unfastened the box. "How kind of you," said the first soldier when he saw the éclairs. I held my breath as each soldier chose one for himself and took a big bite. Then they waved me away, and I ran to Arne's house as quickly as I could.

When he answered the door, Arne looked
surprised to see me. Then he saw the box
and his face relaxed. I was out of breath, but
I managed to tell him about the soldiers. He

opened the box and dipped his fingers into each of the four cream centers.

Out of the last éclair, he pulled a folded piece of paper. He opened it up. It looked like a map with a message scribbled on the bottom. I caught a glimpse of some numbers and the word *train* before Arne refolded the note and stuffed it into his shirt pocket. He smiled at me.

"You did well, David. Thank you." I felt proud. Wouldn't Elsa be envious.

When I got back to the shop, Papa was alone behind the counter, sorting through a pile of receipts. He looked up when the bell jingled. I could tell he was happy to see me. I nodded to let him know I hadn't failed.

Papa said, "I saw the soldiers stop you. You were very brave."

I took a deep breath. "Papa, I know about Rachel."

Papa looked up at me, surprised. Then he nodded. "You did well today," he said, "but we'll talk more about it later." Of course, how could I have forgotten? Even the walls have ears.

He locked the cash register. "David, would you pull the shade down and lock the door, please?"

"Yes, Papa." I went over to the door and locked it. Through the glass I saw the two soldiers walking up the other side of the street.

When they were directly opposite the pastry shop, they both glanced my way. The tall one said something to the other one, and then they both laughed.

I quickly pulled down the shade so it said Patisserie Closed.

"Isn't Rachel eating with us tonight?" I asked as we sat down to dinner.

"Not tonight, David," Mama said. Her voice was very tense. "She's so busy with her schoolwork. She studies with friends until very late. But you know that already." As Mama handed me a plate of vegetables and a small piece of meat, Papa's eyes flashed me a warning. I guessed he didn't want Mama to know about my errand to Arne's house. He didn't speak all through dinner.

That night Papa came into my room to say good night. Finally I could ask him the question that had bothered me all day. "If King Christian loves us, why did he surrender to the Nazis? That wasn't very brave, was it?"

Papa sat on the edge of my bed. He thought for a moment. "There are so many ways of being brave, David. What you did today was brave. The people who work for the Resistance are brave. And King Christian is also brave. He didn't want to surrender to the enemy. But he knew we were outnumbered and unprepared. He didn't want any more Danes to die. He weighed the odds, and they weren't in our favor." Papa shook his head. "It must have been very difficult and painful for him. Doing something difficult can take great courage, David."

"Like when the king had his fleet scuttled?" In August the king had ordered his ships to be sunk in the harbor.

Papa nodded. "It must have broken the

king's heart to sink those ships, David. But he had no choice. He had to prevent the Nazis from using them."

I remembered how the explosions woke me up early that morning, and how I had looked out of my window to see what was wrong. Orange and red flames licked the dark blue sky. Bright sparks flew in all directions like fireworks.

"It's the harbor! The ships are on fire!" a voice rang out.

Our street filled with people staring silently at the sky. Some people were crying. It frightened me to see grown-ups crying. That was another thing I'll never forget.

"So," Papa said, "just remember that our king had to make difficult choices. Soon we too may have to make difficult choices."

What did he mean? What choices? But I was too tired to ask any more questions. My

eyes felt heavy. I heard Papa say, "King Christian always does what he believes is right. We must follow his example."

Papa kissed me good night. Most papas smell of cologne or tobacco, but my papa smells of baking. It's my favorite smell. Before he left the room, he said, "Your mama knows about Rachel, but she mustn't know about what you did today. She has enough to worry about."

I nodded. "I won't say anything, Papa."

It wasn't in the official newspapers. Papa heard it from someone who had heard it from someone else who had read it in one of the illegal newspapers. At breakfast on Sunday morning he told Mama and me. Though he looked at Mama when he spoke, I knew that he was really telling me. "I heard there was a train derailment. Quite a mess, by the sound of it."

Mama looked up from her coffee, her eyes wide with fear. "The Resistance?" she asked. She was thinking of Rachel.

Papa nodded. "They knew the Nazis were sending supplies back to Germany, and they blew up the tracks. It seems the explosion stopped the train. Tipped most of it onto its side, just like a toy." That's when he finally looked over at me and winked.

Mama asked if anyone had been caught, and Papa shook his head. "No, they were very lucky. Whoever was involved got away."

Mama closed her eyes for a moment. "They might not always be so lucky," she said. "They take risks, and for what? So many of them are young people. Even . . ." She didn't finish, but I knew what she was thinking.

"They do it for Denmark," Papa said in a soft voice, and reached out to touch Mama's hand. "They do it for our freedom."

Mama nodded. "You're right, of course," she said. "But it still doesn't help me sleep at night."

Papa kept looking at me, and while Mama began to clear the breakfast things away, he gave me a little nod. So that was it. I thought my stomach was going to flip over like the Nazis' train. Maybe I hadn't set the explosives. Maybe I hadn't crept out under cover of darkness with my comrades. But some-

how, I'd been part of it all. That's what Papa was telling me with his eyes. I ran a simple errand—taking chocolate éclairs and a secret message to Arne—and that's how they knew the train's route and times and everything. Because of me!

For the rest of the morning no one spoke of it again. Mama cleaned the apartment, and I did some homework. In the afternoon we went for a walk, but every time we saw soldiers, Mama clung to Papa's arm and looked so upset that Papa finally said, "I think we should go home now. Besides, I have some things to do in the shop."

As soon as we arrived home, Mama seemed to relax a little.

"I think I'll catch up on some reading," she said, and headed for the living room.

"In that case," said Papa, smiling at me, "we'll leave you in peace." Then he asked me to help him in the shop. "Perhaps we could even bake some cookies for Mama. Who knows, maybe one day we'll be partners? What do you say? Nathan and Son—Patisserie?"

When we were downstairs in the pastry shop putting on white aprons, I broke the news to Papa.

"I want to be a writer, not a baker." Then I realized I might have hurt his feelings. "Besides," I said quickly, "I could never be as good as you. You're the best baker in Copenhagen."

Papa laughed and ruffled my hair. "Well," he said, "it still couldn't hurt to learn a trade, just in case the writing doesn't make you a living right away. Don't forget," he reminded me, "Hans Christian Andersen apprenticed as a tailor before he became a famous writer."

I helped Papa clean the shop, and then

he showed me how to make his famous sugar cookies. They smelled wonderful and tasted even better. As we worked, neither of us mentioned the Resistance or the train. But I thought about it a lot. And I had a feeling that Papa was thinking about it as well. Even though I'm usually only allowed one or sometimes two cookies a day, that day he let me eat at least half a dozen.

"It's your reward," he said. He didn't say what the reward was for. I didn't think it was for helping in the bakery.

Whatever I do when I grow up, one thing is certain. I'll never be a mathematician. On Monday we were taking a math test in class. Math has always been my least favorite subject. I tried to concentrate the way Miss Kiersted always told me to, but my mind kept wandering.

"If a man takes three hours to plant four hundred tulip bulbs . . ." That was a lot of bulbs. Wouldn't he get a backache? Wouldn't he get hungry? ". . . how many bulbs would he plant in four and a half hours?"

Miss Kiersted's voice made me jump. "Class, don't daydream now. You only have ten more minutes." Even though she said *class*, I couldn't help noticing that she was staring right at *me*. My face grew hot, and I looked back down at the page of problems. They still didn't make any sense, no matter how hard I concentrated. What if the man planting the bulbs was tired after the first two hours and worked slower? What if a dog barked and he looked up for a minute, or he was thirsty and had to drink some lemonade?

I glanced over at Elsa. She was writing furiously. Everyone seemed to be writing as if they knew what they were doing. Was I the only one who couldn't solve math problems? I sighed with frustration. In the distance I heard the loud slam of a door, followed by raised voices. One of the voices belonged to our headmaster.

Soon I heard the stomp of boots. Everyone else heard it too. We looked up from our papers. Miss Kiersted frowned at us and began to speak. But she didn't say anything, because just then the stomping feet stopped outside the classroom next door. That class was a grade above ours. I heard the door open and close but nothing else. I remembered that at least three boys in that class worked for the Resistance.

Miss Kiersted went back to marking papers while the rest of us went on with the test. But I couldn't concentrate.

Suddenly the door flew open, and Miss Kiersted jumped. The headmaster stepped into the room, followed by a Nazi officer. We all put down our pencils and stood up as the officer looked around the room. Miss Kiersted stood up very straight behind her desk.

"May I help you?" asked Miss Kiersted. Her voice sounded a little shaky. The headmaster looked very serious. He said the officer had something to say to us.

"We are taking an important test," she said. I hoped that wasn't true, because I was sure I was going to fail it. I saw how Miss Kiersted lifted her chin to make the soldier think she was not at all scared of him. That's what she told us to do when we were rehearsing our play.

The officer looked around the room. He wore a stern expression. "I want to remind your students that it is an offense, a serious offense, to harm any soldier of the Reich. It is also an offense to do anything at all which might prevent soldiers of the Reich from carrying out their duties."

He looked at each of us in turn. When he looked at me, I forced myself not to flinch even a little bit. If Miss Kiersted could do it, so could I.

"Denmark and Germany are friends. Our people are brothers. We are the same race. But those who help criminals to break the law will be punished—even if they are children. Remember that, all of you. I'm sure that our führer can rely on you not to involve yourselves in dangerous matters."

I knew the officer was talking about children who worked with the Resistance. Then I realized with a shock that he was talking about me. Hadn't I helped the Resistance? I wanted to look away, but it might draw his attention, so I stood very still and didn't blink. I tried to think about the man who planted bulbs for four and a half hours.

Then the soldier clicked his heels, first at us and then at Miss Kiersted. He raised his arm in the hated salute. "Heil Hitler!" he said.

Miss Kiersted stood in silence as if she'd

been turned to stone. The soldier waited a couple of seconds, but Miss Kiersted still didn't return the salute. Finally she said, "Good day." The soldier gave her a very nasty look, but to everyone's relief, he turned as if his heels had little wheels on them. The headmaster opened the door. The officer followed him. He slammed the door and was gone.

Miss Kiersted motioned to us to sit down

again. "I will give you all an extra ten minutes to finish the test because of that rude interruption." Her face was very white. We picked up our pencils in silence, and for the next ten minutes the only sound I could hear was that of pencils on paper.

The next day it rained. "Copenhagen is so boring in the rain," said Elsa when we walked home from school. This would have been the perfect time to tell Elsa about my dangerous mission with the éclairs, only Papa had warned me not to tell anyone, not even Elsa.

It was very difficult to keep the secret, but even though the news was bursting to get out, I had made a promise to Papa. And promises must be kept.

We decided to play in the Jensens' living room. Mrs. Jensen was reading a newspaper. Elsa and I sat by the window, looking down at people scurrying by clutching their umbrellas. Two new soldiers were standing together across the street instead of on the corner. One looked up. Why weren't they in the usual place? Were they spying on us?

"I know," said Elsa, "let's play with Vic and Dora!" Vic and Dora were the Jensens' budgies. Their cage hung on a stand in a corner. They weren't all that much fun to play with, although they had a cage full of bird toys. Unlike canaries, they didn't sing, and they rarely talked. Sometimes they nipped my finger with their beaks. I turned away from the window. Maybe the budgies would help me forget about the soldiers.

Mrs. Jensen looked up from her paper. "I've got a better idea. Why don't you two take the cage into the kitchen and clean it out?" That didn't sound like much fun either, but we agreed to do it.

The blue budgie, Vic, was named in honor of the comedian Victor Borge. Dora, the green budgie, wasn't named for anyone in particular. Vic bobbed up and down as Mrs. Jensen placed the cage on the kitchen table. He looked funny, and we laughed.

"Victor Borge made people laugh too," she said as we began to clean out the cage. "He made jokes about the Führer. Hitler put him at the top of his list of enemies. Imagine that. The most dangerous man in Denmark was a Jewish comedian who plays piano and sings funny songs!" Mrs. Jensen laughed.

Before she left the room, Mrs. Jensen reminded us to be careful not to let the birds escape. One time they had escaped, and it took hours to catch them.

Elsa had already taken the old sheet of newspaper from the bottom of the cage. I began to fold the clean sheet that Mrs. Jensen had given me to replace it. Elsa said, "My parents once saw Victor Borge on the stage in a big theater."

I carefully unhooked the budgies' water container and took it over to the sink. "What happened to Victor Borge?" I asked. "Did Hitler have him arrested?"

Elsa shook her head. "No. He escaped to America. I'd like to visit America one day. Or maybe Canada. Papa has a cousin in Toronto. Papa says that if things here get very bad, we should try to find a way to join his cousin in Canada. But Mama says we're like Vic and

Dora, trapped in a cage with the door shut."

"It's lucky my cousin went to England before the war," I said.

I stopped refilling the bowl and looked at Elsa. "You wouldn't really leave Copenhagen, would you?"

Elsa shrugged. She was busy putting the birds' toys in their proper places while Vic and Dora marched up and down on their wooden bar like tightrope walkers in a circus.

"I don't know. I'd rather join the Resistance, but if Papa and Mama went to Canada, I suppose I'd have to go with them." She looked at me. "Naturally, I wouldn't stay forever. Copenhagen is my home."

"Mine too," I whispered. If only the Nazis hadn't also decided to make it *their* home.

We watched the two birds hop about in their nice, clean cage. Elsa sighed. "It's so quiet here," she said. "You'd never know there was a war."

She spoke too soon.

That night both our families were sitting together in the Jensens' apartment. Rachel wasn't there, but no one said anything. My parents had brought over some small cakes from the store. Mrs. Jensen had come across a can of real coffee when she was cleaning out her kitchen cupboard. "It might be a little stale," she told Mama, "but if it's not too bad, you could use some of it for your honey cake."

"That would be wonderful," said Mama.

"But tonight," said Mrs. Jensen, "I want to make a good, strong pot of coffee. Who knows when we'll have another?"

Mr. Jensen laughed. "That coffee must be at least three years old. I can't imagine what it will taste like."

But Mrs. Jensen said it couldn't be worse than the chicory coffee. As a treat, even Elsa and I were going to be permitted a taste of this grown-up drink. Our cups had extra powdered milk in them to make the coffee weaker. "Or you'll be wide awake all night," laughed Mr. Jensen.

As it turned out, we wouldn't sleep very well anyway. We didn't even get to drink our coffee. It all started with Vic and Dora making clicking noises with their beaks. At first we just thought it was funny. Then Vic and Dora got more agitated. They chirped and chirped and flew about as if there were a cat in their cage. Elsa and I laughed. Mr. Jensen frowned. Mama and Papa looked startled. But Mrs. Jensen jumped up from her chair. Her face was very pale.

"Come quickly, everyone! Down to the cellar, now! It's an air raid."

Mr. Jensen protested. "But we haven't heard the siren. . . ."

"Vic and Dora are the only sirens I need," said Mrs. Jensen in such a frightened voice that we all rushed after her as she ran out of the apartment.

We hurried down the stairs to the cellar. It was directly under Papa's and Mr. Jensen's shops. Halfway down we heard the air-raid siren. Above us other doors slammed. Other feet clattered on the stone steps. Neighbors appeared on the landing.

"Oooh!" someone screamed ahead of me.

I'd just reached the
bottom step but
looked up just in
time to see Elsa fall.
She had tripped and
lost one shoe. Mr. Jen-
sen helped her up, and I
grabbed her shoe. There
was a nasty graze on her
knee. It was bleeding a little. She bit her lip but didn't
cry. We all hurried into the
makeshift air-raid shelter.

We huddled in the cold,
stone cellar. The only light
came from one single
bulb on the ceil-
ing and a couple
of flashlights. "I
always keep one

with me, just in case," said an old man from the top floor.

Mr. Jensen had one too. He'd grabbed it from the dresser on his way out of the apartment.

We'd made it just in time. There was a terrible explosion close by. The building shook. Suddenly I was very scared. I snuggled between my parents. Surely the building would collapse onto us at any moment. What if I never got to be a fish in *The Little Mermaid*? Or see my story in the school magazine?

Elsa was dabbing at her knee with a small handkerchief. She spat on it and dabbed some more.

There was another explosion. Elsa winced and hugged her papa's arm.

I thought of Rachel. Was she safe?

"Are they German bombs?" Elsa asked.

Mr. Jensen said they were Allied bombs.

"They're trying to hit German targets, Elsa."

"But what if they kill *us*? We're not their enemy. I thought the Allies were supposed to *help* us." Tears welled up in her eyes, and she brushed at them angrily with her fist.

"They are," said Mr. Jensen. "But I'm afraid it's not that simple. Some things take time. Sometimes innocent people are the ones who suffer most in war."

"That's not fair," sobbed Elsa.

"No," said her papa, giving her a hug. "You're right. It isn't fair."

I must have fallen asleep soon after that. I dreamed that bombs were falling all around me as flames engulfed Copenhagen. The wailing of the all clear woke me up. We staggered out of the darkness and back to our apartments in the pale gray dawn light. On the way upstairs Papa yawned but said there was no time for him to sleep. "I might as well start baking for my first customers."

"I'll help," said Mrs. Jensen. But Papa said she should get some sleep. "I can manage just this once. Come in later when it gets busy."

She didn't argue. When we reached our floor, Mama asked Mrs. Jensen what she meant about Vic and Dora being air-raid sirens.

"Before every air raid they make a big fuss. They fly around their cage and chatter as if it's the end of the world. The first time it happened was three years ago, five minutes before the Nazi planes invaded."

Mama smiled. "That's the first time my life has been saved by a couple of budgies."

That morning Elsa and I walked to school in silence. We passed a pile of rubble that had once been a building. A few people stood around looking lost and sad. I realized with a shock that it could easily have been our building.

In class I could hardly stay awake. Twice Miss Kiersted had to ask me to pay attention. But I wasn't the only one. Most of my classmates also looked very sleepy. Even Miss Kiersted had dark circles under her eyes.

That night after I finished my homework, I went straight to bed. I thought I'd fall asleep right away, but just as my eyes closed, my bedroom door opened.

"Rachel!"

My sister put one finger to her lips and carefully closed the door. She came over to my bed. The room was dark, except for a small night-light. The blackout drapes were securely in place. I could just make out Rachel's face. She looked tired.

"I can't stay, David. I just wanted to tell

you how proud I am that you helped us. Getting that map to Arne was very important."

I could feel my face flush. "Did I help a lot?"

Rachel nodded. That's when I noticed her hair. Instead of letting her braids hang straight down, she had wound them around her head. It made her look older, more serious.

"Arne couldn't send his usual courier. Lucky for us no one suspected you."

"I want to help again," I said.

Rachel hesitated. "I'm afraid it's getting more dangerous, David. We've heard rumors."

"What rumors?" I asked.

"Bad things are happening all over occupied Europe. People are disappearing. Jews, mostly, but other people too. It might happen here."

I couldn't believe that. "Not in Denmark," I said. "The king would never allow it."

"Sometimes things happen that even kings can't stop," said Rachel. She checked her watch by the night-light, then stood up.

"Before I go, David, I have a favor to ask."

"Anything," I said.

"Always listen to Mama and Papa. Do whatever they ask of you."

My heart sank. It wasn't what I had in mind, but I promised anyway.

And then she was gone.

I soon discovered that Rachel was right. There were things that even kings couldn't stop. In the days before Rosh Hashanah the grown-ups didn't speak very much. When they did speak, it was in whispers. Elsa and I couldn't stand it. "Something's going on," she said.

Nevertheless, we had other things to think about. Our class play was going to be per-formed before the whole school at the end of October. We rehearsed for half an hour every day. Miss Kiersted said we were almost perfect, especially Elsa. And after the performance the school magazine would be handed out to everyone. There were some things even the soldiers couldn't spoil.

Elsa and I still walked by Tivoli Gardens sometimes. It wasn't as much fun anymore. The city was quieter, as if holding its breath waiting for something to happen.

Elsa said, "Papa thinks the Nazis are up to something. No one knows what it is."

That night Mama finally made the honey cake. She even let me help. Our apartment smelled wonderful. It was like living inside a gingerbread house.

Five

Copenhagen, September 29, 1943

The morning before the start of Rosh Hashanah, I sat with Papa in the synagogue. I listened to the Hebrew prayers and thought of Mama's freshly baked honey cake. We'd be eating it that night.

All of a sudden Rabbi Melchior stepped forward and held up his hands for silence. The chanting stopped.

"Friends," said the rabbi, "I have bad news. The Nazis plan to round up Denmark's Jews

tonight. We must go home and prepare for our escape. God bless Denmark."

Papa held my hand tightly as we walked through the busy streets. Everyone was in a hurry. I saw anxious faces. News had spread quickly. When we got home, Rachel wasn't there, and Mama was packing. "The Jensens are taking us to their summer cottage in Humlebaek," she said as she bustled about the apartment getting things together. "We'll all have to wear two layers of clothing. Each of us can only carry one small bag."

I felt very uncomfortable in two shirts and a sweater, not to mention two pairs of trousers. When I complained, Mama said, "It's just until we reach Humlebaek. If we take too much luggage, it'll attract attention."

"But what about Rachel?" I asked.

My parents exchanged looks. "Don't worry, she'll be fine," said Papa. "Now let's hurry."

Mama had prepared the dining table for Rosh Ha-shanah. Everything sparkled on the white tablecloth. Silverware, crystal, and china gleamed, ready for the festive meal. A meal we wouldn't eat.

"Wait," said Mama just before we left. She darted back to the kitchen and grabbed the cake tin. "Those Nazis won't get my honey cake," she said.

The streets were crowded. Everyone seemed to have a purpose. There was a strong, unspoken sense of urgency in the air. I kept bumping into strangers. Autumn leaves had begun to fall, but not enough yet for a crunchy brown carpet. Papa grabbed my hand, and Mrs. Jensen took Elsa's.

We had only walked a few yards when I saw a familiar figure in a red and white knitted cap cycling toward us, waving. She hopped off her bicycle and crossed to our side of the street.

"Miss Kiersted!" whispered Elsa. "What's she doing here?"

Our teacher's face was flushed. "I'm so glad I caught you in time," she said in a low voice. She nodded at my parents. "I won't keep you. I just wanted to give David this." She pulled something out of the basket on her bike and handed it to me. "It's the school magazine with your story, David." She smiled. "I printed it up last night. I thought you'd want to have it. Good luck."

Before I could thank her, Miss Kiersted

had hopped back onto her bicycle. "God bless Denmark," she said, and quickly rode off.

"God bless Denmark," whispered Mama.

"Hurry," said Mrs. Jensen. "We have no time to lose."

• • •

The station was as busy and noisy as always. Usually I liked the mix of sounds—the hiss of steam from the engines, the echo of footsteps on the platforms, excited greetings, and hurried goodbyes. This morning was different. Maybe it was my imagination, but there seemed to be more soldiers around. They walked up and down or stood idling about, smoking and talking.

"Don't be fooled," said Papa. "They're always watching. Smile. Don't look nervous."

I tried my best. I thought of how I'd be missing the class play. It was lucky Miss Kiersted hadn't cast me in a lead role. No one would miss one little sardine.

Papa looked around as we headed for the ticket kiosk. "To the Germans it's just another busy day in Copenhagen. Let's hope they don't figure out why it's so busy."

I pasted a smile on my face and told myself I was going to the country for a holiday. Smiling when you don't really want to is harder than you'd think.

Papa bought round-trip tickets for six to Humlebaek. That made me feel better. That meant we'd be coming back, didn't it? When we stepped onto the train, my face relaxed. Elsa didn't look up until we'd found a compartment. Then we both glanced out of the window. A girl from my school was boarding the train with her parents. She was Jewish too.

We settled into the compartment. Elsa and I sat across from each other. I looked out at the station clock. Only five minutes and we'd be off. So many things could go wrong in five minutes. I turned away. It would be better to think of something else. I thought about one of the problems that I'd got wrong on the math test.

If three children each had a dozen walnuts and someone gave one child three more and another child six more, how many would they have altogether if the third child ate two of the walnuts? I concentrated hard. Just when I thought I had the answer, Elsa hissed at me.

"David!" I looked at her. She was staring out the window. I turned to see what had caught her attention and came face to face with a soldier. He was grinning at me. I looked at my parents, but Papa gave me a warning glance. He was telling me not to react. So I turned back to the soldier, smiled, opened my bag, and took out my copy of Hans Christian Andersen's *Fairy Tales*. Pretending to read is almost as difficult as forcing a smile, because you have to remember to turn the pages every minute or so.

Elsa followed my example and also took out a book. Mrs. Jensen was knitting, and

Papa and Mr. Jensen were sharing a newspaper. Mama reached into the bag on her knee and pulled out a tin of lemon drops. "I almost forgot," she said. "David, these are your favorites." She passed around the tin, and everyone took one.

My hands were shaking as I carefully unwrapped mine.

I could see through the corner of my eye that the soldier was still watching us. Even though I was more scared than I'd ever been before, I had to do something. I put the lemon drop in my mouth.

"Mama," I asked, "please could I have another?" It was difficult to breathe, and my voice trembled. Mama looked surprised, but she held out the tin. I took another lemon drop. But instead of unwrapping it, I held it up to the window as if to offer it to the soldier. I smiled at him. At first he looked startled. Then he laughed, shook his head, gave the Nazi salute, and marched off down the platform. Lucky for me I was sitting down, because my knees were shaking.

Elsa had reached down as if to fasten her shoe. "Has he gone?" she whispered.

"Yes," I said.

"Thank goodness," said Mama.

"Thank David," corrected Papa with a smile.

"I have to admit," said Mrs. Jensen, "that was very quick thinking, David." Mr. Jensen nodded and winked at me.

I bit down on the lemon drop. Then I looked out the window again. I hoped the soldier wouldn't get on the train.

As if he'd read my mind, Mr. Jensen said, "Don't relax yet. We're still not out of the woods, my friends."

A few minutes passed, and the soldier didn't return. I was just about to open my book again when the whistle blew. Both Elsa and I jumped. She looked as scared as I felt. Then the train jolted as if waking from a sleep. It began to chug out of the station, gradually picking up speed. I was leaving Copenhagen—my home. Everything in my life was going too fast, just like the train. I looked outside and watched my city fly by. All too soon we left it far behind.

I unwrapped the second lemon drop, popped it into my mouth, and leaned back in my seat.

"Forty-three walnuts," I said to myself. Miss Kiersted was right. Problems weren't so difficult if you concentrated hard enough.

It was dark by the time we arrived in Humlebaek. The cottage was cold and damp. While Mrs. Jensen lit a fire, Mr. Jensen said, "On Saturday a fishing boat will take you to Sweden. Meanwhile, you must stay well hidden."

My heart sank. Sweden? That was another country! We weren't going back to

Copenhagen after all. Papa must have bought the round-trip tickets to fool the Germans.

Mrs. Jensen told Papa, "I'll run the pastry shop until you get back."

I wondered when that would be.

We could only go to the outhouse after dark. The rest of the time we stayed cooped up like chickens in a small back room, hoping no one would find us. Mr. Jensen said that most of the neighbors could be trusted. "But not all," he said. And of course there were always the soldiers.

Saturday arrived, but Rachel still hadn't joined us. I had known all along that she wouldn't.

"Rachel wants to stay and work for Denmark's freedom," Mama told me. I could tell she was trying hard not to cry.

I swallowed the lump in my throat. Rachel was very brave. We'd have to be brave too.

Mama took out the honey cake and cut it into seven pieces. She put the seventh piece back into the cake tin. "That's for Rachel," she said.

Mrs. Jensen smiled and said, "I'll see she gets it."

As we ate the cake, I made my wish for a sweet year.

"I have something for you," said Mr. Jensen. He handed me a package wrapped in newspaper. "A New Year's gift," he said as I unwrapped it.

It was the engine from my train set. The train I'd wanted so much. I didn't know what to say. I opened my mouth, but all that came out was "Thank you." I carefully put the gift in my bag, wishing I had more words. Mr. Jensen seemed to understand.

"Don't worry," he said with a grin, "I'll

save the rest of the train for when you return
to Denmark."

We packed our bags and put on our layers
of clothing again. It was still uncomfortable,
but this time I didn't complain.

Then it was time to go.

"The boat will be setting out earlier than

usual," said Mr. Jensen. "The skipper needs time to get a catch before he returns so it won't look suspicious." We said hasty goodbyes to Mrs. Jensen and Elsa, promising to write. Clutching our few belongings, we followed Mr. Jensen outside.

There was no moon, but the sky glittered with stars. "We'll have to keep low," Mr. Jensen whispered, "if we don't want to be seen."

In minutes we were crawling through a ditch beside the forest. Mr. Jensen led the way. I was next, then Mama, and finally Papa. The salty sea air made my eyes sting. It was cold too. I was actually glad to be wearing so many clothes. We had gone about fifty yards when I heard the crunch of boots on gravel.

Mr. Jensen stopped abruptly. He gestured a warning, and we all lay flat. I held my breath. Two men were heading for the ditch. They were speaking German. I felt my heart thump hard against my chest as I lay on the wet earth.

The men stopped. *"Kalte Nacht, nicht?"* said a voice.

"Ja," said another voice. I squeezed my eyes shut.

"Hast du Feuer?" asked the first voice. I heard the striking of a match and smelled cigarette smoke before something hot fell on my hand. I bit my lip and picked the spent match from my skin. Tears stung my eyes, but I kept silent. Then I heard quick, light steps on the gravel. A familiar voice called out, "Oh, soldiers, soldiers! Please come. Mama heard noises near our cottage."

Elsa!

The soldier who'd complained about the cold muttered a curse and threw down his cigarette. His aim was off this time, thank goodness. It landed on the edge of the ditch a few inches in front of me. It glowed in the darkness. Again I heard the crunch of soldiers' boots, only this time they were heading for the Jensens' cottage. We continued crawling toward the beach. Now the salty air smelled fresh and clean.

There were five other people waiting on the dock. A fishing boat was moored there. As we got closer, I saw the boat's name, *Jette,* in big letters on her side. The skipper appeared, and Mr. Jensen spoke with him, then turned to us. "It's time to go. You must hurry." The other passengers began to board.

"I almost forgot," said Mama, handing Mr. Jensen a scrap of paper. "It's my honey cake recipe for Mrs. Jensen."

Mr. Jensen smiled. "She'll like that," he said. "Now you should go. I'll wait until the *Jette* is safely on her way." There were more thanks and goodbyes before the skipper helped us onto the boat.

The *Jette*'s hold smelled bad. I wrinkled my nose. The skipper laughed. "I apologize," he said, "but this is where I keep my daily catch."

He threw a net over us. "I have eight big fish today," he said. "Please be as silent as herring."

The engine started up. The boat was on its way. In ninety minutes we'd be in Sweden. For the next hour all I heard was the engine's drone and the splash of waves against the hull. I had almost fallen asleep when I heard another boat. It stopped beside us.

A bright light swept over the hold. A harsh voice shouted, *"Achtung, achtung!* What are you doing out so early, fisherman?"

The skipper shouted, "If I don't start out before the other boats, there will be no fish left. Then how shall I feed my family?"

There was silence. We all held our breath. Finally the man in the patrol boat laughed. "On your way, Skipper. Stay out of trouble." Then they were gone.

It was quiet for a long time. Then from far

away I heard singing. The singing grew louder, and Papa said, "Listen, the Swedish people are welcoming us with their national anthem."

From the deck we saw people on shore,

holding lanterns and waving. I stood between Mama and Papa. "What shall we do in Sweden?" I asked.

"We shall live," said Mama.

Sweden, October 10, 1943

Dear Elsa,

   Finally we can send letters through the underground. Thank you for distracting the soldiers that night. Papa says you saved our lives. We live in a hotel in Landskrona. The owner, Mrs. Kasperson, is very kind. She won't take our money. There are many Danish Jews here. They were saved by their neighbors, just as we were. I miss Copenhagen. Write soon.

Your friend,

David

Denmark, November 1, 1943

Dear David,

I'm so glad we fooled the soldiers. When we heard them heading toward the beach, I got scared and ran after them. The soldiers were disappointed not to find anyone. Serves them right. Miss Kiersted said I was wonderful as the Little Mermaid. The play went well, even though we were missing one sardine! She said to tell you not to forget to work on your math problems.

My mama thanks your mama for the recipe. She says that when the war is over, we'll all eat honey cake together to celebrate a sweet year. Speaking of cake, I hope you have a happy birthday.

Every day I look toward Sweden and wave to you. Will you pretend you can see me and wave back? Promise?

Your friend,

Elsa

I raised my hand to wave.

"Yes, Elsa," I said, looking toward Denmark. "I promise."

AFTERWORD

Although *A Time to Be Brave* is fiction, the historical events described in it are true. At first when Germany invaded and occupied Denmark, life was not as bad as in other occupied countries. Adolf Hitler saw the Danes as fellow Aryans. Most Danes did not feel the same way. Danish children were the first to resist.

In 1943 the Nazis planned to deport all Danish Jews. A sympathetic German official named Georg Duckwitz warned the Jewish community. The majority of Danish Jews were saved by their non-Jewish neighbors, people like the Jensens, who helped them escape to Sweden. Later Sweden also welcomed Danish communists, members of the Resistance, and others on Hitler's most-wanted list.

The Jews who were captured in Denmark were sent to Theresienstadt, a concentration camp near Prague. King Christian X and Danish officials kept in touch with them. The Nazis agreed not to kill the Danish Jews because Germany still hoped the Danes would join them as allies. For the rest of the war, Danish officials continued to press for the Jews' release, and the Danish Red Cross sent food packages to them in Theresienstadt.

A Dane, Dr. Johannes Holm, pretended to befriend Nazi officials. He tricked them into signing a paper that ordered the release of 425 Jewish prisoners from Theresienstadt. On April 13, 1945, a convoy of white buses arrived at the camp. The Danish Jews were going home.

By May 8, 1945, the war in Europe was over.

Turn the page to learn how to bake
your own honey cake!

SERVES 8

4 eggs

1 cup brown sugar

½ cup strong brewed coffee, cooled

2 tbsp. oil

1¼ cup honey

4 tbsp. applesauce

3½ cups flour

1 tsp. cinnamon

1 (or 2) tsp. ground ginger

1½ tsp. baking powder

1 tsp. baking soda

2 lemons

1. With an adult's help, preheat the oven to 325 degrees.
2. Beat eggs and sugar in a large bowl until

fluffy. Add coffee, oil, and 1 cup of honey. Blend with a fork. Add applesauce. Blend again.

3. Combine flour, cinnamon, ginger, baking powder, and baking soda in a medium bowl. Add to the egg mixture and mix well.

4. Grease a large pan, or three small pans, with oil. Fill ¼ full of batter.

5. Bake for 45–60 minutes, or until a fork stuck in cake comes out clean. With an adult's help, carefully remove cake from oven, turn out of pan, and set to cool on a rack or plate.

6. When it's cool, poke a few more holes into the top of cake with a fork. Heat remaining honey with the juice and grated peel of lemons until warm. Pour warm liquid over top of cake and wrap in waxed paper or aluminum foil until liquid is soaked into cake.

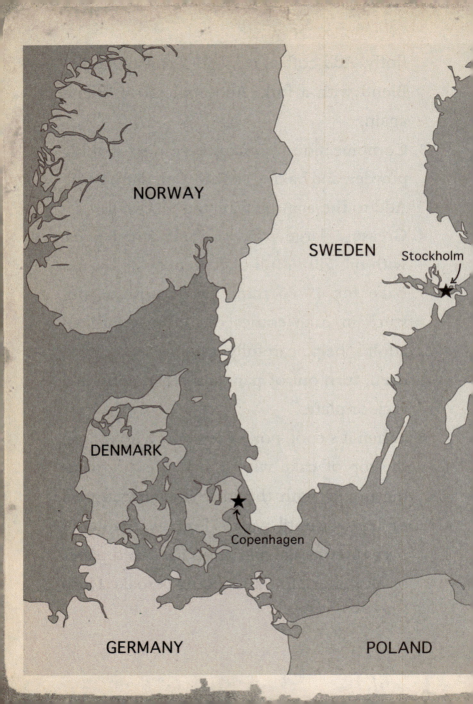

WORLD WAR II TIMELINE

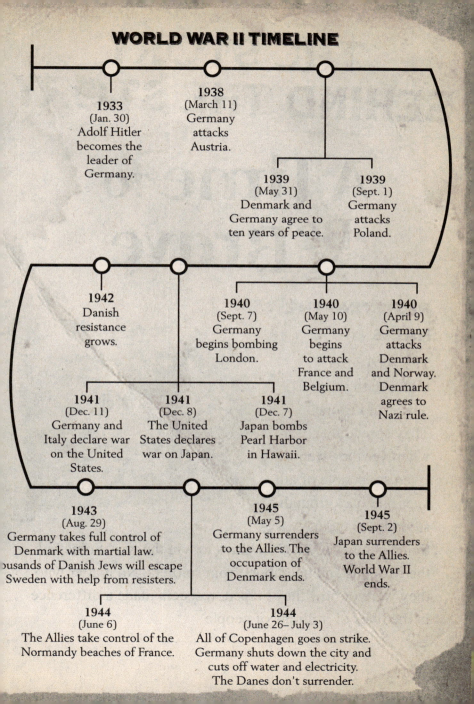

1933
(Jan. 30)
Adolf Hitler
becomes the
leader of
Germany.

1938
(March 11)
Germany
attacks
Austria.

1939
(May 31)
Denmark and
Germany agree to
ten years of peace.

1939
(Sept. 1)
Germany
attacks
Poland.

1942
Danish
resistance
grows.

1940
(Sept. 7)
Germany
begins bombing
London.

1940
(May 10)
Germany
begins
to attack
France and
Belgium.

1940
(April 9)
Germany
attacks
Denmark
and Norway.
Denmark
agrees to
Nazi rule.

1941
(Dec. 11)
Germany and
Italy declare war
on the United
States.

1941
(Dec. 8)
The United
States declares
war on Japan.

1941
(Dec. 7)
Japan bombs
Pearl Harbor
in Hawaii.

1943
(Aug. 29)
Germany takes full control of
Denmark with martial law.
Thousands of Danish Jews will escape
to Sweden with help from resisters.

1945
(May 5)
Germany surrenders
to the Allies. The
occupation of
Denmark ends.

1945
(Sept. 2)
Japan surrenders
to the Allies.
World War II
ends.

1944
(June 6)
The Allies take control of the
Normandy beaches of France.

1944
(June 26– July 3)
All of Copenhagen goes on strike.
Germany shuts down the city and
cuts off water and electricity.
The Danes don't surrender.

THE STORY BEHIND THE STORY

A Time to Be Brave

RESISTING THE NAZIS

The Nazis used violence to seize power in Europe. They spread fear wherever they went. Even so, people of all ages and backgrounds stood up to them.

Some slowed down Nazi plans to win the war. Some hid their friends and neighbors from soldiers. No matter who they were or how they helped, resisters made a difference in the lives of millions of people.

KING CHRISTIAN X

King Christian X was
Denmark's ruler when the
Nazis took over Copenhagen.
He knew he had to help his
people. Every morning, King
Christian rode his horse through
the streets. When the crowds
saw him, it gave them hope.
They felt less scared. He also
tried to keep all his citizens

safe, including the Jewish people. The Nazis wanted to
make laws to take away Jewish freedoms. The king said
no. The Nazis tried to get the king to use his power to
hurt his people. King Christian refused. He never used
violence or fought in the Resistance. But he could have
gone along with the Nazis, which would have been easier.
Instead, he stood up for what he believed in. He helped
Denmark stay strong.

PREBEN MUNCH-NIELSEN

Preben lived in a small fishing village. He went to school
in Copenhagen. Some of his friends were Jewish, but
everyone was treated the same. The Nazis came when
he was fourteen years old. Preben was young, but he

wanted to do something to help. At first, he carried mail for the Resistance. Later, he helped Jewish people escape. He took them to Sweden in his fishing boat. It was very dangerous, but he saved 1,400 people. Finally, Preben had to escape to Sweden, too. When the war was over, he came home.

VICTOR BORGE

Victor Borge loved to make jokes. He was the most famous comedian in Denmark. When the Nazis invaded, two things put him in danger. First, he was

Jewish. Second, he used his comedy to fight the Nazis. Victor joked about them, to show he was not afraid. By making people laugh, he made them brave. The Nazis wanted to arrest him . . . but they were too late. He escaped to America and told his jokes for many years.